Space Kraken

A StarSoldier Chronicle

C.R. Coyne

Feedback

Table of Contents

Also By CR Coyne

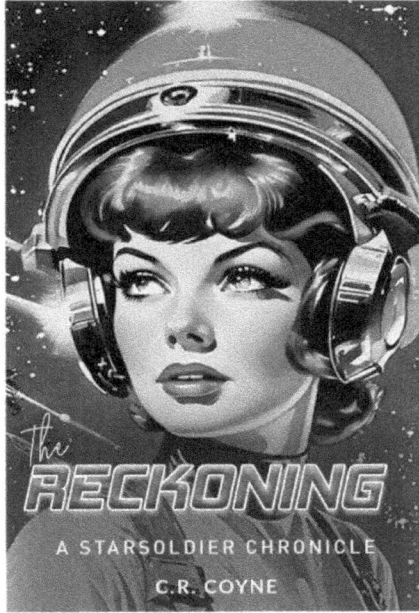

The squad is sent on a routine research op. In and out with no gunplay necessary. No one said anything about saving a dying race. Or leading a slave revolt. But before the squad can call this mission over they'll have to do both! And live to tell the tale.

Buy your copy today!

Also By CR Coyne

Regulus V was a colony of eight billion humans, rich and comfortable in their adopted home. Great place to visit. But when the entire system becomes a wasteland the StarSoldiers must face an ancient evil as old as the stars themselves and stop it before more die!

Buy your copy today!

Galactic Area of Human Sphere

Star Map of Notable Sites

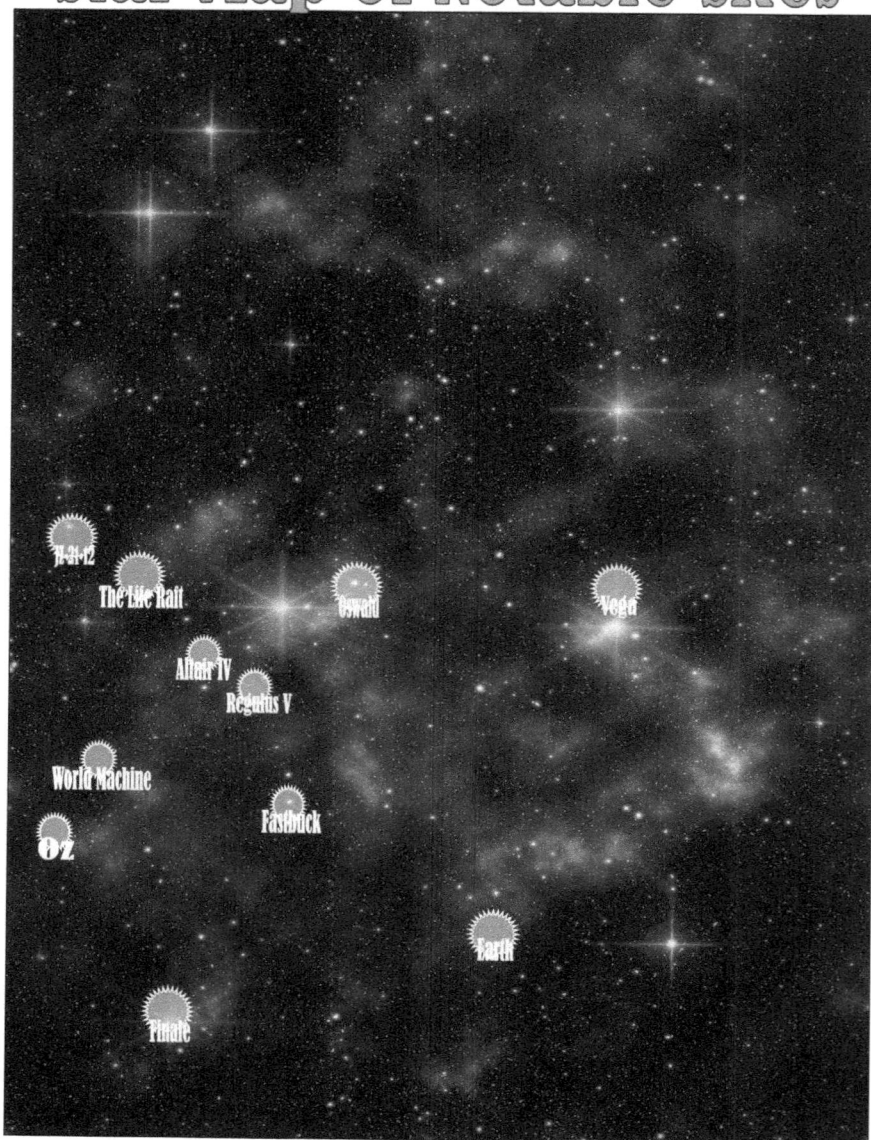

History of the Mohawk Tribe

The Mohawk are traditionally the keepers of the Eastern Door of the Iroquois Confederacy, also known as the Six Nations Confederacy or the Haudenosaunee Confederacy. Our original homeland is the north eastern region of New York State extending into southern Canada and Vermont. Prior to contact with Europeans the Mohawk settlements populated the Mohawk Valley of New York State. Through the centuries Mohawk influence extended far beyond their territory and was felt by the Dutch who settled on the Hudson River and in Manhattan. The Mohawks' location as the Iroquois nation closest to Albany and Montreal, and the fur traders there, gave them considerable influence among the other Tribes. This location has also contributed directly to a long and beautifully complicated history.

In the 1750s, to relieve crowding at Kahnawake and to move closer to the Iroquois homeland, the

French Jesuits established a mission at the present site on the St. Regis River. The Mohawk people had continually used this site at the confluence of the St. Lawrence River Valley as part of our fishing and hunting grounds prior to the building of the first church. "Akwesasne" as it is known today, translates roughly to "Land where the partridge drums" has always been a prime location due to the confluence of several small rivers and the St. Lawrence River.

Space Kraken

A StarSoldiers Chronicle

C. R. Coyne

Leviathan is not the biggest fish;--I have heard of Krakens. Herman Melville

"**M**ust have been vone helluva accident, look at zthat thing!" Dutch says Murphy looks over the readings and shakes his head while pulling on his lip.

"Accidents seldom have such system Dutch. I think something else happened." Sarge says.

"Twenty seconds to contact point," I add in unnecessarily. I just want to be included in the general doom and gloom of the moment. Yeldon reaches past me flips a couple of switches on my readouts and goes back to what she's doing. I grump a little, "don't you have a command station all your own on this bridge?"

"Yeah but I like yours better," she offers as she tracks the debris cloud starting to drift our way. She adjusts the polarizing plates a little to accept bigger impacts without sending every alarm in this ship off.

HARVE gives a hmmm which is usually a bad sign, clears his electronic throat which is worse, and offers "Sergeant Murphy I'm picking up our derelict, I think on my scanners. Lots of readings not making much sense in this soup. I am trying to datalink with the onboards now but so far no dice. They seem off or dead."

"Isn't being turned off kinda like dead?" Striker asks HARVE.

"No, that's just sleeping till needed. These circuits are turned off, stone cold, or destroyed." HARVE defines. I nod knowing what he means, there is very little of the ship left, and that which remains is almost unrecognizable as a spacecraft.

Sarge pulls his lip out to its full extent and says, "ladies and gentlemen may I introduce the latest United Earth warship UES Resistant." No one laughs, truth is Sarge's gentle pun isn't funny and I don't think he meant it to be. It's hard to laugh or even crack a smile while watching Earth's pride hang broken and limp between the stars its loyal crew floating around it like horrible satellites circling its broken shell. "Work your scanners and build me a picture all of you. I want to know what happened." Sarge says then comes over looks over my readouts and asks, "any sign of combat?"

I wag my head left and right on my shoulders, "I really don't know. I mean some readings say yes, others say no. Her tubes were hot, that much I can tell you for certain. If she was in battle she went down with a fight. Other readings say no, but one thing puzzles me. Those aren't bodies out there, that debris is reading organic at least some of it but not human. Also just to make a round dozen mysteries no Transition Unit."

"Destroyed." Sarge offers. That's as much as my Sergeant knows about inter-dimensional transition theory and equipment.

I emphatically shake my head, "couldn't have happened. Not by any law of physics we know. Even if the sphere was smashed into molecules I'd still get a reading. And given enough time, say a hundred years or so those molecules would heal into a fully functional sphere."

"Maybe their attacker stole the sphere?" Sarge asks and shrinks a little at the look I shoot him. "Yeah, gotcha, have to enter multi-dimensions to get it. Nonetheless, it isn't here."

I nod conceding the obvious. "I need to get over there and look around." I offer. "I want a remote for HARVE loaded in. I want to take Yeldon as backup."

"You're just saying that because I took over your station for a minute." Yeldon pipes up a big grin on her face.

I shake my head, "I want you because you can shoot and are cool headed." She subsides the instant she realizes I am serious. Jess then nods saying nothing slips out of her chair to head to the armory.

Sarge looks a few more reading over, "I'd feel a whole lot better sending you over if I knew what you were walking into. But these scans aren't making a lot of sense." He stands looks over the panel a few more times trying to glean something he missed the first fifty times he studied over the data and says "go ahead Yaz. But I want you and Yeldon armed, armored, and on high alert."

As Sarge finishes and gets ready to move on to another scan Mohawk shutters and spins around like a child's toy flinging all of us out of our chairs or off our feet. HARVE chatters something but I can't hear him. The red battle lights illuminate the bridge, and I imagine the whole ship is screaming and bathed in red light. I climb up and shut off the klaxon. I can finally hear HARVE, "We're under attack!" I nod and quietly say dryly "thank you

HARVE we are aware." Sometimes HARVE can be so pedantic. I look over and see Yeldon sprawled face down an ugly red streak stains the door, she must've taken a header right into the doorframe. If I could remember where I keep my legs I'd race over to help instead I flop out of my chair like a dying fish and have to brace against my console. Before I can do anything Striker is by her side. I crawl back to my station and activate every panel I've got. What I see chills me to the bone, "what is that thing?" I announce. Two huge red lights looking for all the world like red eyes stare right at Mohawk like it's a Sunday buffet. Arms tipped with various instruments each more brutal than the last ring what can only be called a mouth. The sinewy body glides through space like a swimming shark in space, sinuously twisting its body around it starts to move toward us picking up speed as it comes on.

Striker offers, "I'm picking something up though I'm not sure it's from the Resistant. This power signature is familiar, I can't place it. But I've seen this before." Striker adds then plows back into his plates and starts looking at our attacker.

Sergeant Murphy climbs into his command station and starts to look over the same data I'm getting, he commands Dutch, "get 'em hot!" Dutch starts to flip switches even before the order is out of his mouth. He turns to me, "release control to

Dutch." I do so knowing she can out fly any two me's on any given day. "Tell me what you're seeing corporal?" Serge asks me and I try to analyze and think faster than I ever have before. The Mohawk banks hard to port as Dutch does a pretty Immelman throwing the ship around and bringing our tubes to bear on the nasty whatever it is. She fires a full salvo at point blank range, the red streaks race from underneath the ship and strike the...the big ugly space monster thing. I watch each strike, debris erupts from the surface sending bits and pieces out into space. If that were a ship it would be blown into dust. But unfortunately, this isn't a ship, anyway not the way I define a ship. As the answers start to flow into my readouts I lean back and blow out my air in a noisy whoosh. It's as close as I get to cursing..."You are not going to believe this," I start out as Sarge turns back from Dutch's panels to face me.

II

Sarge listens carefully to everything I have to say which isn't much on the whole I realize once it's out. But his eyes narrow when I finally admit, "all my readings say the thing is mechanical, but it's not just a machine, it's alive as well. And if all that isn't enough, half the time my scanners say that thing out there isn't there. I can't explain it."

"But you can see it during those scanner blackouts?" Sarge asks and I nod affirmatively.

Dutch joins in with, "attack has no lasting effect, sir." Her Universal as cold high and white as her bone china complexion. Before Sarge can say anything another blast sends us hurtling away from the Resistant and again we spin and do handstands on the bridge as the ship flies uncontrolled into black void. I look around at the crew and notice both Striker and Yeldon are missing. He must've taken her to sickbay. I see Dutch holding onto her console and taking the stick for manual maneuvers. That actually makes me feel better even if it's not supposed to. She rights the ship slides to starboard, then curves us around and snaps off three shots at such close range the thing can't maneuver away in time and she catches it on the side. Again more debris flies off the hull slash body and again seems to do nothing but annoy it as it fires back. Dutch slips under it and tucks us close to the belly. The seeking weapons miss us and race away into the void then disappear.

Sarge murmurs, "I hate this ride." Then turns back to me and asks "where's the power supply for it?"

I shrug my shoulders as my attention is captured by one diode reading after another. It takes a second or two but I suddenly realize how unmilitary that answer is and before Sarge can give me the drill sergeant stare I follow up with something useful. "I don't know, but I'll tell you one thing, I've found Resistant's Transition Unit." And I point at the very center of the machine-creature. The unit's strange light show can be glimpsed flashing in a kind of recess or pit, ringing this depression are waving tentacles that reach into the night like they're trying to grab us. Strike that, they are trying to grab us!

As I work furiously I catch Yeldon gingerly walking onto the bridge a pressure bandage on her head. Her eyes are dilated and unfocused. Sarge looks over at her and she nods. "I'm okay, I can do my job." Striker is right behind her and adds "within limits. Limit one, no giving backup for two weeks." I figured as much. But my problem has now changed from investigating the Resistant to landing and investigating the monster ship.

"I'll go myself," I state flatly.

Serge cuts me off at the knees, "no you won't. I will go with you. You still want HARVE on remote?" I nod yes.

"Sir I can go," Yeldon says her voice clear and loud. Striker gets ready to object but Jess waves him off. "I can handle it. I've worked with a hangover before."

Serge looks over at Striker who shakes his head. "I need you and Dutch here, I need me and Yaz over there..." With that Murphy and I make our way to the launch bay.

III

Sarge and I take the penance it has room for two fully armored humans to sit in the cockpit. The shuttle doesn't. Sarge pilots us to what we guess is the main superstructure or should I say what is left of it after Dutch's kind attentions. The thing does not seem to understand we are close or more likely doesn't particularly care. That thought gives me the heebie-jeebies. We set down about a thousand meters from the Resistant's sphere close enough to see the waving tentacles not close enough for them to grab a hold of our ride home. Cycling the airlock I open the hatch and set foot with all the care you do when walking through a minefield. The body of the thing is a kind of alloy. Nothing I have ever scanned or for that matter dreamed up before. Some of the elements aren't on our periodical table. I look at the artificial horizon from end to end and it's only now starting to sink in how big this thing is. A blue haze permeates the entire structure.

"I feel through my feet a pulsing sensation." Sarge comments through the microlink.

I nod then realize he can't see the gesture, "the heartbeat." I say and Sarge shakes his head in wonder.

"Really?" He finally asks me. I just shrug.

"HARVE gives me a readout on its power supply," I ask and I hear the whirring sound of HARVE starting to go to work. Sarge and I pull out hand scanners and I set probes on the skin as we walk our way toward the pit.

We get about halfway there when the Tenticles start to reach out at us. Like everything else around this neighborhood it's only as we get close I realize just how big those arms are. "The good news is the tentacles are too big to pick us up. Even at their thinnest part." I report then place another probe.

"Bad news is they can squash us like a bug," Sarge adds.

"Yes, they can do that," I confirm and take more readings. I lean over to put down one of our mobile remotes known as a bug. A neat piece of human engineering, looks like a mechanical's conception of a tarantula but packed with scanners and a nifty processing system that can link up with HARVE, the powerpack can last eighty years. Which, is just about how long it would take for the bug to walk all the way around this monster-ship. The small green flashing light tells me the bug is talking with HARVE and it starts to wander away. I turn around to set another down when I hear

Sarge's Type-10 scream in my pick-up. I shoot my head up and see Sarge sighting his barrel at something to our left. Looking that way I see four angry metal squids shaking their tentacles for all their worth at us and firing some kind of weapon at us that looks like a shrimp fork only four feet long. "You just can't make up days like this", I think as bullets or whatever they're using go whizzing past my head. I get up on one knee sling around my rifle ready to fire back when something knocks me flat on my stomach. I hear Sarge grunt in my pick-up and I push him off and roll out from underneath. I get back on my knee take careful aim and plug one of the uglies right in the middle of what I assume is its head. It spins around throwing half its tentacles out in a squid's imitation of a man dying after being shot. Assuming I got him is my first mistake. The thing rolls a couple of times and I move on to the next target and plug it only to see the first target get right back up with half its body missing and start moving at me again. In the time it takes for me to finish target one off by blowing it to pieces, the other three get close. I'll never be able to stop them all. Thinking fast I reach around my webbing and find a flash grenade strike the bottom of it hard on the funny alloy and toss it. I shut my eyes and even through my blacked-out visor I see the light as it flashes. I open to see my attackers wandering around bumping into each other trying to find their bearings. One steps onto a plate painted yellow just to its left which snaps open grabbing tentacles reach out and the creature is pulled inside. If you could hear sound in a vacuum you'd hear that guy's scream all the way back at Command Central on Earth. I don't waste time watching the show. I heft Sarge and beat feet to the penance and close us up and lift before cycling the atmosphere is complete.

Once spaceborne I check over Sarge and find a nasty wound in the center of his chest. The wound is large, ugly, and deep. "Striker!" I call into my pick-up and get nothing back but static.

"HARVE keep trying to raise the Mohawk, medical emergency," I say as I strip off Sarge's armor.

"I have been trying but nothing," HARVE answers and goes back to work. I look through the viewport and see the Mohawk hanging just outside. The funny thing is it looks just like it did when I took off. I lick my lips and ask the sixty-four dollar question of HARVE, "are we moving?"

"How upset would you be if I said not at all?" HARVE gives back.

"Very," Is all I manage to say, not wanting to hear the worst.

"Okay, in that case. Not very much." HARVE says.

I pull off the Sergeant's helmet and strip off his remaining blood stained armor one piece. I pull down the medical lifebed from the wall unit and using the power assist in my suit lift him gently onto it. He's in great pain, that much I can tell by his thrashing around. I end up putting restraints on his arms and legs.

"Do you think that's a good idea? You know how he feels about medical." HARVE asks me.

"He keeps throwing himself around like that HARVE, and the bullet could shift. Get me, Striker. I don't care what you have to do."

"You just might, we're being jammed. To punch a message through I'll have to use all the power of the penance. That means lights and life support too."

"Do it, I'll put Sarge on the bed's power supply, and keep my suit on while we talk." HARVE is as good as his word and in a few moments, I get to Striker. But I really wish he hadn't. "You have got to be kidding me. I'm a grunt Striker, not a medico." I plead.

"Nevertheless, if he's going to live you have to take the bullet out."

"I could kill him!" I say exasperated with how this conversation is going.

"And if you don't he dies by default," Striker tells me but he needn't I knew that already. But fishing around another man's guts is above my pay grade. "I'm going to walk you through the procedure. You're going to be fine."

"You're just saying that hoping it's true," I murmur but Striker picks it up.

"No! You can do this Yaz, I've seen you work with the circuit paths. Now take the scalpel and switch the power to level three. That's enough to cut flesh and tendon."

I nod and do as I am instructed. An hour later the small offensive metal slug is lying in a jar and Sarge has as neat a suture as I can make. It'll have to do until Striker can get to him.

After that, I tuck Sarge into bed and head back to the cockpit to see if I can perform surgery on whatever is holding us in place. HARVE and I find the tractor that's keeping us in place.

IV

"You suppose we could race in and pick them up then race back out before we get caught?" Yeldon asks Dutch but the gentle smile from the pilot says everything that needs to be said. "Gotcha Dutch, probably not." Yeldon throws herself back into the command chair and looks helplessly at the penance not one kilometer from the Mohawk and herself helpless. "We're so close now I can't understand why they haven't bothered us yet. Just the penance."

"Ve might be able to use the tow cables but I don't know which is stronger, that beam or our cables. I've never seen anything like that tractor beam's power signature." Dutch says then goes back to her readings.

Yeldon looks out and tries to send her thoughts across the void, "we're coming boys just hold on." She says in a stage whisper then goes back to her station and starts to run through options. Problem is they're the same options as before, and they couldn't work the first fifteen times she ran through them, and all that does is make the entire squad find enforced silence their only refuge.

That is until Striker gives a hearty "Ha!" A huge smile taking over his unhandsome face. His eyes twinkle and his broken nose twitches. "I knew there was something familiar about the power signature..." Striker hits a few more controls and his smile only grows bigger.

"Are you going to let us in on za secret?" Asks Dutch finally.

"Fish! Or in this case marine cephalopods. That thing out there is the biggest Squid there is. I've been looking at this all wrong. It's not an energy signature that I am reading, it's bio-rhythm waves. The machine implants in the creature have been throwing me off this whole time."

Yeldon looks at Striker not sure how this new information helps any, "okay where dealing with the universe's largest calamari dish. And?"

Before she's done Striker has left the bridge and races to his lab. Dutch frowns as she watches Striker race out and swears she hears giggling. Maybe that's good news?

Dutch wanders down to the lab and sees Striker racing through his supplies to pull this flask or that beaker of noxious liquids out. Dutch waits about five minutes as she watches Striker start to mix some combination of chemicals that smells like a cross between burning rubber and old fish. After throwing in the last ingredient which turns the potion black, Striker turns to Dutch with a smile, "I need you to get close to that creature."

"How close? Close enough that it can smell that concoction and run away?" She offers wrinkling her nose.

"More or less. I need to be able to put this stuff on the body of the creature."

"Vhat may I ask is…" unable to come up with a good noun Dutch uses "stuff?"

"The same chemical that Earth cephalopods create to confuse predators. If I am right and nothing so far has indicated to me I am. But then again nothing has said I'm wrong either. But if this works…" Striker looks up and sees Yeldon step into view.

"But if it works what?" She asks. With Sarge and Yaz off the ship, she's in command.

"I think I can get that creature to forget all about our penance and start chasing us. I'll need you Yeldon to fire the tow cable and Dutch to keep us just out of reach."

"How certain are you that..." Yeldon wrinkles her nose and then swallows her lunch back down. "That stuff will work?"

"I'm not. It's just a theory. A guess." Striker says and pleads with his eyes for Yeldon to approve. If she says no he doesn't have any ideas for getting Sarge into the sickbay.

"How is Sarge Doctor?"

Striker thinks that over carefully, "he's stable."

Yeldon wrinkles her nose again but it isn't the smell that's bothering her this time. "That's no answer Marko and you know it. How is the Sarge?"

"He needs the sickbay. The lifebed will keep him in suspended animation. As long as the power holds out. Which is about two maybe another three hours. But he's not getting any better."

Yeldon stands stock still and considers every possibility, especially the one where they lose both men. "Did Yaz make any mistakes?"

"Not one. The job was as good as it could be done under the circumstances. Still, I need that man back here to treat him."

"Marko the thing is, if you're wrong..." Yeldon starts out but Striker nods furiously and interrupts.

"They both die and maybe we do too. I know. But in my opinion Ma'am this is a risk worth taking." At that Marko just steps back, he's done all he can to persuade.

Yeldon leans against the bulkhead and considers. She didn't want command, in fact, she's spent most of her career avoiding it like the plague. But now. She looks over at Dutch.

"I don't zhink you should. Sarge has a couple more hours on the bed. Let's vork a few more figures. Get a feel for this thing. Whatever it is."

"If after those two hours, we know no more than we do now then what?" She asks no one in particular then nods. "Striker get ready. Dutch take the helm. We're going to give it a try."

V

I fiddle with some knobs, and pretend the dials are showing me something encouraging every time I adjust something, who am I kidding? They haven't shown me a thing. The penance is stuck and her power supply is drained. The lifebed is still ticking away and I have another hour on my suit. I've lost HARVE which is no help at all. I look out the forward plates and see the Mohawk firing up her main engines and starting to drive right at the monster ship. I shake my head and shout, "no! Just get out of here." But of course, they can't hear me. It's not worth the Mohawk to rescue the Sarge and myself so I can't see why their suddenly getting combative.

But the Mohawk plows forward and settles into a spiral course which sends the ship underneath the monster. I lose sight as they dive under. I speculate on what they're doing but my guesses are no good. With power down, I don't have HARVE or scanners to try and figure out their play. So I do just what I have been doing, sit and watch. I look at the edge of the thing I can just make out the glow of Mohawk's engines as she starts her run toward us.

But instead of trying to chase down or attack the Mohawk, the thing slides forward toward me, then goes in reverse like it hit a force field. Next, it cants to starboard and swings away from Mohawk and the penance its drive bright blue as it burns a straight line trying to get away from us. "Ya!" I shout and start jumping up and down and laughing as the thing slips away from us. Mohawk positions itself to fly close and overhead. In seconds I feel rather than hear the dull thud of the tow cable as it strikes home and I can feel the penance starting to move as the Mohawk drags it away. In seconds we are a full AU from the monster-ship. The main bay doors break open and I am sucked up inside like a pea in a straw. I feel the gentle bump as the penance is put in its cradle and I lose all sense of motion. I cycle the hatch and see Yeldon attaching an emergency power lead to the penance. Striker pushes past me and gets Sarge on a stretcher, switches the thing to hover mode, and pushes his patient out.

Yeldon steps into the penance and starts to download the data I have collected. I step back inside feeling somewhat underappreciated. "Can I give you my thoughts?" I ask. Yeldon nods to me. "That thing is more alive than machine.

"We know that. Striker figures it closely resembles something from Earth an enceph.."

"Cephalopods," I supply.

"Yeah, that thing," Yeldon says.

"Okay, well what you may not know is it has at least two maybe more little Cephalopods. Whether they're crew or children or who knows what I can't say. But they are armed and able to stand vacuum. That's what got Sarge. Not robots as I first thought."

"What changed your mind?" For the first time, Yeldon turns to face me and listens intently.

"I've had plenty of time to think things over...The way they kept coming at us. It was intelligent. They knew they would lose folks, but on they came. Not in a machine way, if you know what I mean. Mindlessly moving forward regardless. They used the fact it would take more than one shot to bring them down to get at us. I'm just lucky. Anyway, we have to know why it wanted the Resistant's sphere and we have to know what its next plan is."

Yeldon with ill-disguised relief says, "conveniently you're in command. So what's your orders?"

"You've been just waiting to say that huh?" She smiles and shrugs.

"Pips aren't my style." Yeldon says simply and turns back to download the remainder of the scans I took."

"I want to search the Resistant. I want to understand how the sphere was stolen. That might lead us to why. Also, we need to see if anyone is still alive over there. It's a real long shot. But we've got to check."

"You ah, up for another penance ride?" Yeldon asks a twinkle in her eye.

"Are you able? That bump on the head is bleeding." I say pointing to the red smear on her forehead bandage. She nods and I head out to replace my powerpack and Yeldon suits up.

In twenty minutes we are ready. We haven't seen hide nor hair of the creature. That's Striker's preferred name and I adopt it as monster-ship takes longer to say. Yeldon and I climb into the penance and I cross my fingers this will be a quicker trip. We fall away from Mohawk and creep over to the Resistant. Our slow speed is meant to not disturb the space kraken just over the horizon. "Now I know how the Greeks felt," I say and Yeldon laughs.

We keep our eyes open, or in this case our passive sensors on alert and make it to the broken hull of the Resistant.   The biggest feature of Resistant at this point is the huge hole that sinks almost twelve decks in the middle of the ship showing the violence and strength it took for the creature to get the sphere. I try not to think about that level of power if it's turned on the Mohawk. I find an emergency airlock and dock sealing the penance to it. Yeldon and I arm up and step out to a scene of devastation the likes of which I cannot comprehend all in one take.   Bulkheads are smashed and parts of ship are strewn all over the place. But no bodies, at least not so far. The ship is of course dark its power cells drained and never to be re-charged because the ship's sphere is gone. Jagged holes peer out of deck plates walls ceilings just about everywhere. Dutch clicks over on our pickups and asks "Anyone alive?"

I shake my head and say "As far as we can tell the creature dug its way into the hull of the Resistant and tore out the sphere with main force. So far no bodies, they might've been sucked out of the ship. No, that doesn't make any sense, too many of them for that to happen to everyone. You have to be here Dutch to understand but it's obvious that no one could have survived this kind of attack. It was too fast, too violent. Here I'll click on my vid-feed to you but I doubt it will give you a complete idea." I can hear Dutch and Striker both gasping as they look over the images. I point my lead to the ceiling of the engineering deck so both get a pretty picture of the stars that shouldn't be shining through the ceiling. As we talk over events I turn to Yeldon and say, "I keep getting a clicking sound on my pick-up. Are you hearing that?" She listens to her feed frowns and shrugs her shoulder plates at me. But I know I am hearing something, a steady regular pattern that won't stop. I dismiss the problem for now and admit to all and sundry "to tell the truth this is a dry hole. I don't know why I bothered."

Yeldon puts a gentle hand on my shoulder, the armor detects the touch and sends a signal to my brain. Otherwise, I'd never know she's there. I turn to her and she smiles, "you came here looking for survivors. That was a good gesture no matter how it turned out." Funny but I do take comfort in that as we head back to the penance and leave the ghost ship behind. As we move toward the Mohawk that clicking starts coming back into my pick-up. I have nothing better to do so I start to listen and try and decipher the signal.

"HARVE can you detect this noise or signal I'm getting?"

I wait as HARVE hums and snaps then says, "it is there. It's familiar. Let me..." and he trails off then comes back, "it's a transmission but I can't for the life of me tell where it's coming from." I have to smile at that, only HARVE the immortal machine could use that phrase with such feeling.

I start tapping the clicks out and start to notice a pattern. "Da, Da, Da, dum…" And find myself singing along with the clicks. "Who would be playing Beethoven to me in deep space?" I ask no one in particular as it's too crazy a question to even pose. I grab a stylus and pad and start writing the notes down. As I start to get intrigued Yeldon is putting the penance down in the Mohawk. She gets up and exits as I sit there scribbling away. A picture begins to come clear. "No," I say out loud even though I know I am alone. Even HARVE has left me be as he supports the mission as it stands. I listen and listen and write and write like a madman. "It can't be…" I mutter and keep writing then look at the power gauge on my suit. It's a little over half. I'll just have to risk it. I close ship fire up the engines and swing the bay doors open and leave like a thief in the night. I tap HARVE and order him to create a remote and off we go.

HARVE is humming happy to stretch his diodes out again, he loves to travel. Breaking in on my thoughts he asks, "where are we going?"

I wince at that, he isn't going to like this. "Back to the creature. I know where those clicking are coming from."

HARVE goes silent for a few seconds and says finally, "your funeral." Nice.

I pilot the penance in a wide sweep, the thing is not far away. Just outside scanner range is my guess. We sweep the area it was last in and find nothing. Not a surprise. Then we reverse and head in an untravelled direction. After flying for half an hour I pick up its bulk on the scanner. "It must be asleep and forgot to turn on its cloak." I quip.

HARVE asks, "then you're certain it's a mechanical?"

"Nope, just the opposite," I say unhelpfully but at the moment what I need is to get to the creature and land right where I was before. As we get close I can see the thing start to switch on, the weird Transition Unit lights always aglow but are more violent and colorful when they're operating. The creature swings into an attack course, but slowly, and sluggishly. I just keep barreling in on it aiming for my landing site near the sphere. The thing tries a number of maneuvers but does not fire at me. I keep waiting for the sky to explode with my death along with my craft. But while the thing moves with all the aggression of a killer shark it doesn't launch a single weapon at me no matter how close I get.

I do a loop and at the apex cut my thrust allowing the penance to be pulled down by the artificial gravity of the creature. I skim a few dozen kilometers and land no more than a meter from my last LZ. "HARVE stay frosty and alert. I'm going out." I pull out a small hand device.

HARVE recognizes it right off, "you took us all this way just to talk to our probes? We could've done that back at the Mohawk."

"No, we can't. Not this probe." I start looking around and find the mobile running toward me. I have to grab it and get it into the penance and onto data support as it were, that is physically linked with HARVE. Once its batteries start to recharge it begins to chatter away at a speed my handheld can't comprehend. But HARVE can.

"It keeps asking for help? What more can we do for it? Give it hot cocoa, tuck it into bed?"

"The probe isn't talking to us HARVE, it's the creature. Once it understood the nature of this little guy it began to call out to us." I lean back and just now start to realize the enormity of the problem I have just teased out. "You remember those little goons we fought when the Sarge caught a packet?"

"Vaguely," HARVE says insulted by my question.

"What if I told you those things kidnapped this creature? And further they are forcing it to attack."

"Touching. It still hammered the Resistant. Look at the size of this thing Yaz, and don't go all dewy-eyed on me. If it wanted to not kill, I think it is more than big enough to say no. It's still the enemy. "

I look at the mobile probe and shake my head at HARVE who picks up the motion and grunts at me, which annoys me. Sometimes he's too human. "No HARVE, somehow those creatures are controlling this being. We need to help. That is what we do help people."

"People, Yaz. You know humans." HARVE reminds me.

"Nothing in the regs defines who we aid HARVE and you know it. We have got to free this animal or allow its owners a free passage into human space. Then we really will need help. There was a reason they wanted that Transition Unit. And it wasn't to go sightseeing."

HARVE grumbles for a second then asks, "granted it needs help, how do you plan on helping? This thing is huge!"

"By letting it die," I say with a finality that I believe comes along with the statement.

"You're an expert on this thing's life cycle?" HARVE ask. HARVE at this point must think I'm off my rocker.

"By overloading the Transition Unit."

"Maybe it doesn't want to die?" HARVE asks reasonably.

But again I have an answer, "that was what the message said HARVE. Help me die. It took me a while but I am sure that is the message. We have to get to that pit. And set the sphere on overload."

"We have to do that do we?" HARVE asks wryly.

VI

Pain. Followed by a blaze of pain that sets the teeth on edge and the body twitching and twisting to try and get away from the source of the pain. But every turn and twitch brings more pain. The agony was both physical and mental. The pain would not go away. It did not matter if he obeyed the pain or not, there would be more pain. And that led to dark places. Dark thoughts that left him empty and alone. Life was to be lived, to experience an open universe, endless skies, and endless wonders to behold. A life of pain and a solitary existence was not life.

VII

Sean Murphy awoke with a start. His chest explodes and his eyes tear up and he settles back into the lifebed and re-learns how to breathe. Striker comes in and looks over the panels and clucks his tongue then smiles that kind of smile only doctors can get when you have to follow their orders. "Now let that be a lesson to you. Lie back and be happy you're alive."

"How long was I out?" Sergeant asks knowing all along that whatever the amount of time it was too long.

"Six hours. You owe Yaz your life. He got the slug out while you two were on the penance."

"He can perform surgery?" Sean asks wondering if his guts are in the right places.

"He can when I tell him what to do."

Sean lays back when a tingle hits his mind. A gnawing itch invades his mind, tugging and tormenting. "Torment," he says out loud.

"Yes well, you will have discomfort for the next few weeks. But due to my superior skill, you won't even have a scar."

"Not me, where is Yaz?"

"He went to the Resistant then took off with HARVE on remote to only the space GAWDS know where."

"Get him on the blower," Striker begins to object but is cut off, "Now Marko this is a question of life and death.   Ours and others as well."   Even wounded and laying in a lifebed Sean Murphy had the power of command.   Striker goes to the com-panel and starts a search for Yaz only to find static. "Keep tryin' Doc until you get something."   Sean orders "anything."

End

I stand on the creature's surface and get ready to head toward the pit holding the sphere. The Transition Unit is creating an artificial aurora borealis over the whole creature. I sling out my rifle and get ready for battle. My hope is to reach the pit unnoticed, if I can do that and overload the unit, it won't matter if I am discovered after. HARVE is with me downloaded to a hover rig. The skin; I suppose it's skin or some such; is studded with pipes, bulges of machinery, etc. that I use for cover. I look and all of these are driven into the body of the creature. I try to imagine a torture of a million pins in my body and can't. Thankfully.

We make it halfway; longer than I expected before being seen. A squad of the mini-squid crewmen armed with those dangerous shrimp forks of theirs starts marching toward me. This time I'm ready, my Type-10 is set on contact explosion and I don't hesitate to open fire. One of the brutes goes down after taking a shot to the head leaving nothing but the equipment and a puddle of goo. I race around a huge machine that is thumping under my feet peer out and start to fire again. As I do so the thumping gets heavier. Whatever this thing does, it doesn't like weapons. The squad of aliens whatsits start to flank me but won't fire. The machine must be explosive. I pull away least one of my shots sets it off. I have bigger fish to fry.

HARVE is programmed not to harm any life form and thus stays clear of me as I do the killing bit of our partnership. I race toward the pit when one of the crew gets a lucky shot on HARVE's hover rig which explodes. HARVE is fine he's just transmitting from the Mohawk. I tuck roll and up on one knee blast a hole the size of a bowling ball into the thing and it drops dead. The last three begin to wonder if it's worth taking me on and one decides against it and starts to retreat. His two buddies keep coming, but at least the odds are better. After five minutes of hide and go kill I make it to the pit. Looking into the depression I find that the creature stole the whole rig, sphere, cradle, and controls. That makes this so much easier. I go to the ignition and phase coordinating panel and start setting a doomsday bomb setting. Shots begin to fly around me but I can tell they are careful shots. I knew they would be. But I don't relent and in minutes the sphere is counting down its last seconds in one piece for about a hundred years or so.

I climb out of the pit on the other side and watch as the sphere goes wild. I smile grimly to myself and say quietly to the creature, "won't be long now..."

HARVE breaks into my benediction, "Yaz, I have Sarge he urgently needs to talk to you."

"I'm a little busy right now." I offer as I dodge shots that are landing all around me. I need to find a way back to the penance. "Tell him to get ready to drive as soon as I am aboard..." A familiar voice cuts me off.

"Have you set the sphere to overload?"

"Good guess," I say in a breathless voice as I race around another pillar to take shelter on my way back home.

"Don't! Discontinue that's an order."

"What? Are you nuts?" I start out and again I am cut off.

"Yaz listen to me. I've been in contact with the creature. It doesn't want to die."

"With all due respect Sarge, I was very careful with my translation. I know what it said."

"You know what it said, not what it meant Yaz. It can't say no. It doesn't know how." Sarge's voice sounds almost like pleading mixed with command.

"Great," I say wryly, "my dream date is a giant space fish." I look around and see two more squads of bad guys starting to close in. "What does it want?" I ask into the pick-up as I keep on the move. This time back to the pit.

"Disconnect the sphere. Then next to the sphere is a large machine stuck in its flesh. That machine is facing the bow of the creature. Blow that up. It's the crew's life support." Sarge instructs as I dodge a few more bullets unhelpfully flung my way.

"Yeah, I saw that coming in. Hold on..." I roll as shots ricocheted all around me. I snap off a shot that blows one of the crew to pieces. Two more start shooting at me as I make the ledge of the pit and I dive in. I pay for the leap with a dislocated shoulder when I land on my armor plate wrong. Nevertheless, I keep moving forward and manage to get back to the panel. Stepping around the cradle I see a crewman trying to figure out the panel. He sees me and turns and for one second we lock eyes. Then I squeeze off a round that blasts the critter to pieces. I reverse the overload tout de suite. It'll take time for the unit to cool off, but the sphere won't hold energy anymore and thus won't blow. I have to do some fancy footwork getting out and away from the pit. But the crew helps a little by closing in from every side except the bow. I make it to the life support machine and place three hand grenades on it. Then I start to run as fast as power-assisted armor and a dislocated shoulder will allow. The penance is just in front of me when two plug-uglies step out and point very nasty weapons at me. I dive onto the skin and roll as rounds explode around my helmet. I have no time to fire back, I get up and run hard with my head down straight at the two leaping into the air on power assist and slamming my feet into the left hand thug, and my rifle butt into the other. Both stagger away. I get to the penance hatch and leap inside. I waste no time cycling the lock, just straight to the cockpit and off this kraken I go.

As I pull further and further away I see a bright point of light turn into a globe of pure fire and envelope a quarter of the surface of the creature's back, but this is nothing compared to what I had originally planned. The blue haze fades and the thing lies inert in space. Pieces of the machinery begin to fall off one by one but the sphere and the tentacles attending it are very much alive. I take that as a good sign. But what do I know from Space Kraken? I glide the penance around to the back to see a huge eye looking at me if anything...fondly.

"Yaz! Yaz answer me that is an order." I snap back to reality and answer slowly Sarge has been trying to raise me. "You can land, where the life support system was. I shrug my shoulders and comply. I haven't been in the driver's seat since we first saw this thing. As I begin to set down I see...people. Not just the crew of the Resistant but colonists, spacers, miners you name it. They gather in wonder as I land and get out. No one seems to believe I am here, but all are hoping I am.

Three Days Later

The huge liner Luxor settles into orbit around Oswald. Yeah, we gave the big fish a name. Kraken didn't seem to fit. And "the creature" seemed way too cold. He seems content with the name and has been most hospitable, keeping our people safe and supplied until we could get them home. That turns out to be a bit of a move, there are over two thousand folks from all over in there. The natural arrangement of Oswald's insides has been changing back to original and he's starting to look more himself. That's hard to explain but I like it better. Turns out he only looked like a Kraken because that's what his captors looked like. He had been captured as a baby barely two miles long at the time and made to serve them. More or less they were pirates and they used Oswald not only as a ship but as their main weapon of intimidation.

"Hey, are you listening to me?" Yeldon asks me and I shake my head and turn to smile at her and pretend I am listening. "Why did they want the sphere?"

"The one thing Oswald could not do, and in fact the pirates didn't know how to do was fly faster than light. When they analyzed the Resistant they just about wet themselves."

"They go to the little squid's room?" Yeldon asks a laugh in her eyes.

"You take my point."

She nods but keeps smiling at me. "You're going to miss him huh?"

"I've grown to like Oswald yeah. I'm not the only one getting sentimental. Sarge feels the same."

"He's not the only one." Yeldon offers.

I switch on the com and set the special frequency that Oswald can pick up, "you sure you won't stay? We can protect you and the human sphere is big. Lot's to see. And, we'll miss you."

I get a burbling sound which I have learned is Oswald laughing. "I'll be around for a while Yaz. But there is so much to see, so much to learn! I will never forget humans...and I will come back Yaz, I promise."

Feedback

Please leave honest feedback.
Your opinion is important to me!

Beta Readers Wanted

Do you like to read? Be a beta reader for me! Just email your request...

Email

---

cr.coyne@yahoo.com

Looking forward to hearing from you! Please email your desire to be a beta reader.

COPYRIGHT

© copyright C.R. Coyne 2024

The Reckoning

A Starsoldiers Chronicle

C.R. Coyne

"It just seems like everything is trying to kill you...it's not. It IS going to kill you."—Sergeant Galicky Advice *for Starsoldier Survival Class 102A page 81*

Jess Yeldon licks her pretty lips looks out of the clearforce panels and shakes her long red braids. "I hate space battles..."

I cheerfully pipe up, "this isn't a combat op. We get close check it out and report. In and out no killing along the way." I thought that was quite logical a response.

Jess has different ideas, she just shakes her head again and repeats, "I hate space battles."

Murphy steps onto the bridge with a crisp clean uniform and attitude and we snap to attention. He takes a peek out the clearforce panels for himself, shakes his head, and mutters, "I hate space battles."

I roll my eyes saying "geez! Doesn't anyone have faith in Earth Intel?"

Dutch tips my hat off my head and asks "do you?"

I pick my cap off the deck take a look at the menacing shape just outside the window and decide I don't. Murphy clears his throat and we all stand rigid and ready for the briefing.

"Earth Intel wants us to give a complete outside report on the object. Next, we enter said object and give a complete report on that. That is all."

"Well, at least the briefing is short." I then ask "does Earth have any information on that thing?"

"Good question corporal, yes they do. It's here. Now get to work." Murphy says to me and I jump to realizing any more questions will only get me cleaning induction jets with my toothbrush. So I sit at my console and start to run a series of scans using every wave band of light known to man. After two hours of steady work, I lean back in my chair with a harrumph and ponder the readings. Or in this case lack of readings. Murphy paces back and forth from one station to the other waiting for one of us to give him something useful. But the bridge stays absolutely silent. I finally decide that cleaning induction jets is better than this and pipe up, "I'm not getting a thing on composition. According to my readings that thing is not there."

"I am getting nothing as vell," Says Dutch the frustration in her voice. "This, this," and to add emphasis to her statement she starts to shove her hand at the clearforce panel in front of her "thing isn't real. I can't even tell you how big it is." My boss looks back at the object and starts to scratch his beard. He's been trying to grow the damn thing for two weeks but he hasn't gotten past stubble at this point. And it makes him look like Poncho Villa.

"How did Earth even know this thing was here?" Yeldon pipes up. A good question.

"Tramp freighter spotted it and reported the object to Finale," Sarge says as he keeps looking at the plates.

Looking over at Striker he cocks his head but Marko just shrugs his shoulders. "I wouldn't even recommend trying to land on it. I mean we might step out into open space." With that pleasant thought, Marko falls silent.

"I'm open to suggestions," Murphy says and Yeldon perks up.

"We could fly around it if nothing else we could just keep track of how far we go around it. There's size. The holo-cameras are useless, I've been snapping away at it for two hours and I have exactly zero useable shots..."

"Good idea Yeldon, suit up," Sarge says nodding.

"That's vhat you get for vulentteering informations," Dutch says a twinkle in her eye as Yeldon heads to the launch bay. Girls can be really mean.

In a few minutes, we see the two man gig start its slow progression around the long equator of the thing, for lack of a better term. The thing is hardly round. I keep my eyes glued to my panels as the gig worms its way around. I set a clock timer and using a base of Yeldon's speed I start to figure a few things out. All of which ends up in a whistle escaping my lips as she crawls at full speed back to its starting point. "That thing is twenty miles in radius," I report then start to watch as Yeldon starts to fly a circuit around the poles. I have a hunch and as she rounds the north pole I nod my head. "Twenty miles right on the button."

The speaker crackles to life and Yeldon's voice comes over, "how big?" Because of my answer she gives her own whistle and then says, "it is pitted and damaged in many areas. All impact damage. My guess is this thing has been out here a long, long, time."

"Is your impression we are dealing with a real object or a holo?" That's Sarge trying to figure out his next move.

"I've seen better holos than this. No, I hate to say this but It's…"

"Yeldon?" I call into my pick-up and then shout Yeldon!" I start to adjust madly and I can hear the rest of the squad doing the same thing. Murphy comes over calmly and looks over my readings. I blink in confusion and look up at Sean, "she's gone. I can't find a single trace."

9 798223 831013